SHORT TALES

GREEK MYTHS

IKARUS

Adapted by Dan Mishkin
Illustrated by Rick Hoberg

GREEN LEVEL

• Familiar topics

• Frequently used words

• Repeating language patterns

BLUE LEVEL

• New ideas introduced

• Larger vocabulary

• Variety of language patterns

PINK LEVEL

• More complex ideas

• Extended vocabulary

• Expanded sentence structures

To learn more about Short Tales leveling, go to www.abdopublishing.com

Adapted Text by Dan Mishkin
Illustrations by Rick Hoberg
Colors by Wes Hartman
Edited by Stephanie Hedlund
Interior Layout by Kristen Fitzner Denton
Book Design and Packaging by Shannon Eric Denton

Library of Congress Cataloging-in-Publication Data
Mishkin, Daniel.
  Icarus / adapted by Dan Mishkin ; illustrated by Rick Hoberg.
     p. cm. -- (Short tales. Greek myths)
  ISBN 978-1-60270-136-6
  1. Icarus (Greek mythology)--Juvenile literature. I. Hoberg, Rick. II. Title.
BL820.I33M57 2008
398.20938'02--dc22
                              2007036068

THE GREEK GODS

ZEUS:
Ruler of Gods
& Men

ATHENA:
Goddess of
Wisdom

HEPHAESTUS:
God of Fire
& Metalworking

HERA:
Goddess of Marriage
Queen of the Gods

HERMES:
Messenger of
the Gods

HESTIA:
Goddess of the
Hearth & Home

POSEIDON:
God of the Sea

APHRODITE:
Goddess of Love

ARES:
God of War

ARTEMIS:
Goddess of
the Hunt

APOLLO:
God of the Sun

HADES:
God of the
Underworld

Mythical Beginning

In Greek mythology, Daedalus was a famous architect, inventor, and craftsman. His name meant "cunning worker." He was able to make many things. He made statues for the palace and for public places. He made all manner of machines. He even made toys for children.

Daedalus's homeland was Athens. For a short time, his apprentice was his sister's son Perdix. When Daedalus feared that the boy had more talent than he did, he murdered him. He was then banished from the city.

Daedalus fled to Crete, where he began to work at the court of King Minos. In time, he had a son named Icarus.

Daedalus of Athens was a great craftsman.
He was also a clever inventor.

But he was sometimes too proud of the things he could
do and make.

Daedalus was happy in Crete. He found many uses for his skills. He married and had a son.

They called him Icarus.

Minos was the king of Crete. He showed favor to the clever craftsman Daedalus. One day King Minos found a special project for Daedalus.

King Minos wanted a prison from which no one could escape. He wanted Daedalus to design and build it.

The prison was meant to house a strange creature called the Minotaur.

The Minotaur was part human and part bull.

The people of Crete greatly feared him.

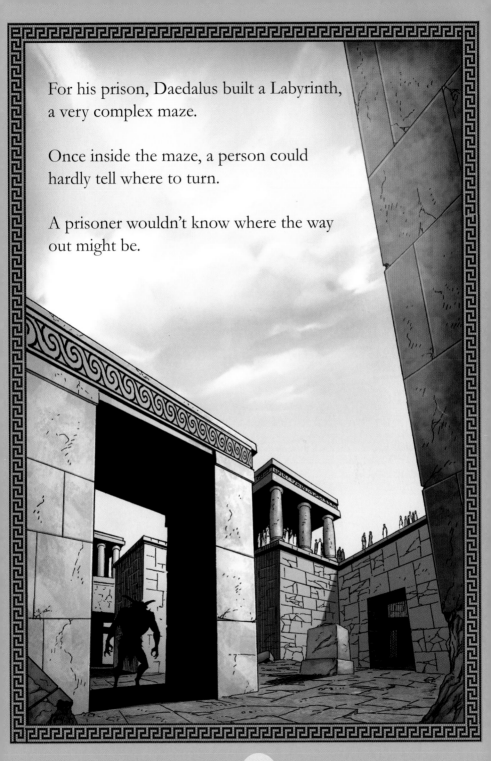

For his prison, Daedalus built a Labyrinth, a very complex maze.

Once inside the maze, a person could hardly tell where to turn.

A prisoner wouldn't know where the way out might be.

As Icarus grew up, he learned to help his father in his work.

And Daedalus had much work to do.

After several years, Daedalus asked the king to allow him to take time off.

But King Minos refused.

The island of Crete had become a prison to Daedalus.

There was no place on the island that King Minos did not control.

Daedalus could find a boat and try to get away by sea.

But, the king's fast ships would surely overtake him.

Then Daedalus came up with a plan.

Daedalus decided to find a way to build wings.

And with those wings, he and Icarus would flee the island at last.

Soon, Daedalus completed his design for the wings.

Then, he and Icarus gathered what they would need to build them.

They collected feathers large and small.

And they went to the hives of honeybees to gather beeswax.

Once the materials were gathered, they returned to the workshop.

Daedalus built a wooden frame for each set of wings.

Next, he sewed the larger feathers directly to the frames.

Then, he used the beeswax to hold the smaller feathers in place.

After many weeks of work, Daedalus had two sets of finished wings.

The wings looked like they belonged to giant birds.

Icarus had seen his father make many wonderful creations.

But these wings were the most amazing of all.

In the dark of night, Daedalus and Icarus went off.

They took the wings to a secret spot.

There Daedalus tried out the wings for the first time.

He rose off the ground, as easily and freely as a bird.

The next morning, Daedalus and Icarus prepared to leave Crete.

They carried their wings out to the shore, avoiding the patrols of the king's men.

But before they took off, Daedalus gave his son a warning:

He must not fly too low. The sea spray might dampen the wings and make them too heavy to fly.

And he must not fly too high. The heat of the sun might melt the wax that held the smaller feathers in place.

Once again, Daedalus beat his arms against the air.

Icarus copied him and found himself lifted up.

Daedalus rose higher, taking off into the sky and Icarus took off after him.

They were flying!

Icarus was full of wonder. This was the world as the birds saw it, a sweeping view of land and sea and sky.

It seemed like the whole world was his to command.

They flew on for a long time.

Icarus forgot his father's warning.

He flew higher and higher toward the hot, bright sun.

Daedalus called out to Icarus.

He tried to remind him of the danger of the sun.

But Icarus was too far away to hear.

And he did not notice when the wax began to drip.

As the wax melted, the smaller feathers of his wings fell and fluttered away.

Icarus knew he was in trouble now.

He beat his arms harder to try to stay aloft.

But all his beating would not help him.

Icarus began to fall, tumbling down, down, down.

His father watched it all happen, but he could do nothing to stop it.

Icarus dropped like a rock.

He plunged into the sea.

Daedalus flew down as low as he dared to.

He circled the spot where Icarus fell.

He searched for any sign of his son and cried out his name.

Then he saw feathers float up to the surface of the water.

Daedalus wept at his son's fate.

After several days, Icarus washed up on a nearby island.

Daedalus dug a grave and buried his son.

He named the place Icaria.

Daedalus flew on to Sicily, where he built a temple to Apollo, the god of the sun.

He hung up his wings in the temple.

They would always remind him of Icarus.

WITHDRAWN